Carol Roth

Little Bunny's Sleepless Night

Illustrated by Valeri Gorbachev

SCHOLASTIC INC.

New York Toronto London Auckland Sydney
Mexico City New Delhi Hong Kong

To Mark, Wendy, Glenn, and Larry
with love—and to the new love
of my life, Jacob Douglas—C.R.

To my parents—V.G.

ISBN 0-439-08115-7

Text copyright © 1999 by Carol Roth.
Illustrations copyright © 1999 by Valeri Gorbachev.
All rights reserved.
Published by Scholastic Inc., 555 Broadway, New York, NY 10012,
by arrangement with North-South Books Inc.
SCHOLASTIC and associated logos are trademarks and/or registered
trademarks of Scholastic Inc.

12 11 10 9 8 7 6 5 4 3 2 1   9/9 0 1 2 3 4/0

Printed in the U.S.A.   14

First Scholastic printing, September 1999

The artwork consists of pen-and-ink and watercolor
Designed by Marc Cheshire

Little Bunny had no brothers or sisters.
He had his very own room with his very own bed.

But sometimes he got lonely—so lonely that he couldn't fall asleep.

One night he thought: What I need is the company of a good friend.

So he hopped next door to his good friend Squirrel.
"May I sleep here tonight?"

"Of course," said Squirrel as he welcomed him in.
Tucked all snug in bed next to Squirrel, Little Bunny
thought how lucky he was not to be alone.
"Good night, Squirrel," said Little Bunny.
"Good night, Little Bunny," answered his friend.

Falling asleep was easy, but staying asleep was not. Little Bunny was soon awakened by C-R-U-N-C-H, C-R-U-N-C-H, C-R-U-N-C-H!

"What's that noise?" he asked as he sat up in bed.

"It's just me cracking acorns," said Squirrel. "I always have a little snack in the middle of the night."

"Well, thanks for having me, but I can't sleep with all that noise!"

So Little Bunny left and hopped some more until he reached his good friend Skunk.

"May I sleep here tonight?"

"YES! YES! A HUNDRED TIMES YES!" shouted Skunk. "No one has *ever* asked to sleep over before!"

Afraid Little Bunny might change his mind, Skunk quickly pulled him inside.

"This is fun," Skunk said as they got into their beds.

Shortly after, they fell asleep . . . but not for long.

Little Bunny was soon awakened by a terrible smell.
"What smells?" he asked as he jumped up.
"I'm afraid I do," said Skunk. "I forgot someone else
was in my room. I got scared and sprayed."
"Well, thanks for having me, but I can't sleep with
that smell!"

So Little Bunny left and hopped some more until
he reached his good friend Porcupine.

"May I sleep here tonight?"

"Certainly," said Porcupine. "You take my bed and
I'll sleep on the floor."

"Yippee!" shouted Little Bunny as he climbed
into Porcupine's bed and bounced around with
excitement.

"O-U-C-H!" he screamed. "What do you have in here?"

"It's just my quills," said Porcupine. "I lose some every now and then."

"Well, thanks for having me, but I can't sleep with those prickles!"

So Little Bunny left and hopped some more until
he reached his good friend Bear.
    "May I sleep here tonight?"
    "Why sure, make yourself at home," said Bear.
    By now Little Bunny was so tired he just curled up
on the floor and went right to sleep.

But very soon after, Little Bunny was
wakened by a loud rumbling noise.
   Oh, no, it's thundering! he thought.
   But it wasn't thundering at all. His friend
Bear was snoring!
   "Well, I can't sleep with that snoring!"
said Little Bunny.

So he left and hopped some more until he reached his good friend Owl.

"May I sleep here tonight?"

"Why yes, if you want to," said Owl. "Just follow me."

An exhausted Little Bunny went right to sleep, but soon he was wakened by a bright light shining in his eyes.

"PUT THE LIGHT OUT!" he shouted.

"I can't," said Owl. "I stay up reading every night. That's how I got to be so wise."

"Well, since you're so wise, could you please tell me how I'm ever going to get some sleep?"

"That's easy," said Owl. "Just go back home where you belong."

Little Bunny took his wise friend's advice.
Too tired to hop, he dragged himself home.
His bed never looked so good to him before.

He jumped right in.

"How wonderful!" he said to himself as he snuggled down. "No crunching noise, no terrible smell, no prickly quills, no snoring, and no bright lights. Just me, by myself, and peace and quiet. Now I can fall asleep!"

And that's just what Little Bunny did!